CAPTAIN
PUGWASH
and the WRECKERS

Also available:

CAPTAIN
PUGWASH
and the WRECKERS

JOHN RYAN

F

FRANCES LINCOLN
CHILDREN'S BOOKS

Text and illustrations copyright © John Ryan 1984, 1986
The right of John Ryan to be identified as the author of this work has been
asserted by him in accordance with the Copyright, Designs and Patents Act,
1988 (United Kingdom).

Captain Pugwash and the Midnight Feast
first published in 1984 by The Bodley Head Ltd
Captain Pugwash and the Wreckers
first published in 1984 by The Bodley Head Ltd
Published in one volume in 1986 by Puffin Books

This edition published in Great Britain and the USA in 2010 by
Frances Lincoln Children's Books, 4 Torriano Mews,
Torriano Avenue, London NW5 2RZ
www.franceslincoln.com

A catalogue record for this book is available from the British Library.

ISBN 978-1-84780-026-8

Printed in Croydon, Surrey, UK by CPI Bookmarque Ltd. in January 2010

1 3 5 7 9 8 6 4 2

Contents

PUGWASH
and the
MIDNIGHT
FEAST

It was a warm, sleepy afternoon on the
Pacific island of Rummi-Tummi
and at the end of a long
and tiring journey,
the *Black Pig* lay at
anchor in the bay.

High on the poop-deck, Captain Pugwash was
peacefully asleep in his hammock . . . or rather,
he was *pretending* to be peacefully asleep . . .

. . . pretending, because at the other end of
the ship, he had noticed that his crew were
behaving in an exceedingly
suspicious manner. For one
thing, they were awake
instead of having their
afternoon snooze—

and the fact that Tom the cabin boy was with
them made the Captain even more worried.

"Now, mess–mates," said the Mate. "We must make sure all our preparations are in order . . ."

9

And in spite of their warnings, Tom climbed
down into the dinghy.

Soon he was rowing to the shore of
Rummi-Tummi Island . . .

. . . and two hours later, safe and sound, and
with a heavy boatload, he was on his way back.

But Barnabas was right—
the Captain *was* suspicious.

Indeed, when he climbed
into bed that night, he
kept all his clothes on!

At first, all was quiet
on board the *Black Pig*.

Then as eight bells
struck for midnight . . .

. . . the pirates jumped straight out of their
bunks and gathered round the mess-table to
enjoy their carefully prepared . . .

... MIDNIGHT FEAST!

"My goodness, you've done us proud this time!" said the Mate, as they surveyed the table. It was spread with all sorts of tasty foods and

delicious island fruits and vegetables.

"Aye, and there's plenty of it too!" said Willy happily.

"Lucky we didn't ask the Captain," said Barnabas. "He'd have eaten the lot—and all by 'isself too!"

"Indeed, Pirate Barnabas . . ."
said a voice from the door.

And there, as the pirates turned in
confusion and surprise . . .

. . . stood their Captain,
looking particularly
pleased with himself.

"Plundering porpoises!" he cried.

"I suppose I ought to put you all in irons! Or maybe make you write out one hundred times:—

"'We must *not* have midnight feasts on board ship!' But no . . . I feel unusually kindly today!

"So, instead of punishing you, I shall JOIN you!"

"But . . . but . . . but . . ." cried the Mate anxiously.

But Pugwash was already
happily tucking in and for
the pirates there was
nothing to do but make the
best of it. After all, he
was their Captain.

Soon everybody was busy eating and pouring out drinks and proposing toasts.

GOOD HEALTH!

And nobody noticed that some *more* uninvited guests were coming to the midnight feast . . .

. . . guests whose ship had
dropped anchor close by
that evening, under
cover of darkness . . .

. . . and who were now scrambling up the side of the *Black Pig*. They were the most unwelcome guests of all—

—Cut-throat Jake and his desperate band of bloodthirsty buccaneers!

Captain Pugwash had just helped himself to
a second scrumptious sandwich
when suddenly—

—Cut-throat Jake and his gang rushed in and surrounded the pirates.

HAH!

"'Avin' a midnight feast, eh?" roared Jake, "and never thought of askin' *us* to join you? Well, we're 'ere now, you greedy old ruffian, and we wouldn't *dream* of not askin' you to join *us*!

23

"Tied up, you'll be, where you can watch *us* finishing off your fancy goodies! And after that it'll be the plank for the lot of 'ee . . . so the sharks can have *their* midnight feast too!"

And very soon Jake had Captain Pugwash and the Mate and Barnabas and Willy and Tom all tied together back to back—

—and dumped on the mess-table, so that they
could all see their captors hungrily gobbling up

all the food in sight.

And so, for the *third*
time that night . . .

. . . a merry party was under way on board the *Black Pig* . . .

. . . so merry that again nobody noticed . . .

that yet *more* uninvited guests were
on their way.

Two great canoes had
approached silently from the
island and the islanders who
came in them were now
silently scrambling up the
sides of the *Black Pig*.

Suddenly the foc's'le was filled with leaping, yelling figures who seized Jake and his crew.

They untied Pugwash and the Mate and Barnabas and Willy and Tom and carried them all out, struggling and kicking . . .

up on to the deck, down over the side of
the ship, and into the two great canoes

in which they were then swiftly propelled
towards the beach.

The whole attack had happened so suddenly
that at first the pirates were stunned. Only
Tom didn't seem to be particularly surprised
at the turn of events. Then Barnabas spoke:

"If you ask me, mess-mates," he said, "the
real midnight feast is taking place on shore
tonight. And you know wot could be on
the menu? . . . Pirate pie and chips!"

"Coddling catfish! They can't!" cried the
Captain.

"Can't they just," muttered the Mate.

Tom didn't say anything, but it looked as though Barnabas was right. Up on the beach hundreds of islanders were gathering round a big fire with a large cooking pot on it.

"Let's hope they'll cook Jake first," whispered Pugwash.

Soon the whole party was set ashore on the beach. "Maybe he'll give them such indigestion they won't fancy any more!" said the Captain.

But Jake and his men were led away to a large hut some distance off . . .

. . . whereas Pugwash and his crew were taken up to a high throne on which what looked like the King of the island was sitting.

When they got there, wreaths of flowers were placed round their necks.

"Garnish! that's what that is!" grunted Barnabas.

And Captain Pugwash became so terrified that
he cried, "Let us go at once, I say! I demand
to see the British Consul! I . . . I . . ."
But the King interrupted him
with a broad smile.

"My dear Captain,"
he said, "what on
earth is troubling
you? There's no
need to look so
anxious.

"It's like this.

When I met your cabin
boy Tom on the island
this afternoon, he told me that a midnight
feast was planned for this evening and
I thought what fun it would be to prepare
a really splendid banquet for you here
on the island, as a surprise.

"And that is what we've done. I'm so sorry that we had to board your ship and bring you back here in such a rude manner. But the arrival of that ruffian Jake—who your cabin boy tells me is one of the vilest villains afloat—left me no choice. Never fear, I shall keep them under very close guard tonight and hand them over to the proper authorities in the morning."

And so, as Jake and his crew crouched
miserably in their prison hut, cursing and
swearing and not having the slightest idea
of what was going to happen to them . . .

Captain Pugwash and the Mate and Barnabas and
Willy and Tom the cabin boy settled down . . .

. . . to the most delicious dinner they had ever eaten in their lives.

"Goodness me!" remarked the King. "What a fearful noise your enemies are making!"

For by now the yelling and cursing from Jake and his crew could be heard all over the island.

"I shouldn't worry too much about them," said Captain Pugwash happily.

"They have probably got some *extraordinary* idea that they're being kept in store specially . . .

. . . for breakfast!"

PUGWASH
and the
WRECKERS

"Fill up everybody's glasses, Landlord!" cried Captain Pugwash. "The drinks are on *me* today!"

There was an astonished silence. The scene was the Buccaneers' Arms where it was well known that the Captain was far too mean to stand a drink to anybody!

But today was different.

"You see," went on the Captain, "I am for once working for His Majesty's Government! Tonight the good ship *Black Pig* sets forth to the Indies with the greatest load of silver bullion ever to leave these shores. And why? . . . because the Navy ship contracted to do the job has been delayed and the silver is needed urgently to pay our gallant soldiers. We sail tonight on the eight o'clock tide, me hearties. Let us drink to a successful voyage!"

Unseen in the snug-bar next door, Cut-throat Jake, the Captain's worst enemy, held out his tankard for a filling of free rum, and chuckled . . .

CHEERS!

"Successful voyage indeed," he growled to his mates. "Ho, ho, ho! He'll get no further than the Barnacle Reef if *I* have anything to do with it! Gather round, lads, and listen to me plan. We have no time to lose! No time even to return to the *Flying Dustman* . . ."

Now the Barnacle Reef lay at the mouth of the harbour. Many a ship had been wrecked on its dreaded, razor-sharp rocks . . . so many that a great light-house had been built on the Reef to warn vessels at night to steer clear.

And it so happened that the keeper of the light-house was none other than Tom the cabin boy's Uncle Joe. In fact, as Pugwash and his crew returned to their ship, and Jake and his men sneaked away to their longboat . . .

. . . Tom had gone to take tea with his Uncle Joe in the living-room of the light-house. They were old friends and it was a chance for Tom to say goodbye to his uncle

GOOD TO SEE YOU, TOM, ME BOY!

before setting out
with Captain Pugwash
on the journey to
the Indies.

"And now, Tom," said
Uncle Joe, "before you
go, I'll take you upstairs
and show you the
light-house lamp."

So Tom followed
his uncle . . .

. . . and when they got upstairs, he was shown
the huge oil light which had saved so many
ships from wrecking on the Barnacle Reef.

"Usually," said his uncle, "I light the lamp by hand when dusk comes down. But if for any reason I have to be away until later, I have worked out a timing device. I have this candle which will last for one, two or three hours. When the candle burns down it sets fire to this short length of fuse which in turn lights the wick of the lamp, at any time I want it."

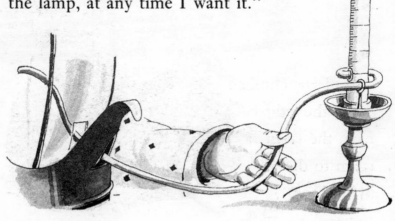

Suddenly Joe broke off. "That's funny," he said. "I thought I heard voices downstairs. It sounds as though we have visitors. Wait now, while I go down and see."

And Joe climbed down the ladder from the lamp room to the living-room . . .

. . . straight into the clutches of Cut-throat Jake and his desperate band who had just arrived in their longboat. In a moment they had him tied up and lashed to his own chair.

"Now, Mr Light-house Keeper," growled Jake, "stay quiet, and you'll come to no harm. But there's some that will, ho, ho, ho! for when dusk comes down tonight, there'll be

no guiding light on the Barnacle Reef
—'cos *you'll* not be able to move to light it.
There'll be a false light lit by a friend o' mine
further out to sea.

And that means
that any ship . . .

(and there's
one *very special*
ship . . . ha, ha,
harhh!) that sails from
the port tonight will smash
on the rocks as sure as eggs is eggs!

"Now that ship belongs to that old
ruffian Pugwash,
and it has a very
special cargo aboard—
a cargo o' silver bullion.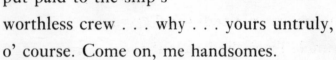
And guess who'll
be waiting on the
rocks to grab it and
put paid to the ship's
worthless crew . . . why . . . yours untruly,
o' course. Come on, me handsomes.

Let's finish off the tea.
We'll need our bellies
full for the dirty
work ahead!"

And the ruffians were so busy
gobbling down what remained
of the crumpets and cakes

that they never noticed Tom's signal
to his uncle from the hatch above . . . nor
Tom's escape down a rope *outside* the
light-house . . . and they heard nothing as he
rowed himself quietly back towards the harbour.

Meanwhile, on board the *Black Pig*, Captain Pugwash was trying to get his ship under way to catch the evening tide. "Cast her off!" he cried. "Hoist the sails . . . Make for the open sea!"

"But I can't remember how to untie the knots," complained Willy.

"I'm in a bit of a tangle meself," grunted Barnabas.

"Fact is, we'll not get nowhere without Tom!" said the Mate. Which was true. Tom really was the only one who knew how to work the ship.

"Weeping walruses!" cried the Captain angrily. "Where *is* the wretched boy?!"

But Tom hadn't gone straight back to the
Black Pig from the light-house. For one
thing he wanted to see where Jake had moored
his ship in the harbour.

The sun was setting behind the
Barnacle Reef when at last he brought the
dinghy back to his own vessel.

AHOY THERE,
BLACK
PIG!!

"Tom! Thank heavens you're — I mean where on earth have you been?" The Captain corrected himself angrily. "We can't wait all night, you know!"

"Sorry, Cap'n," said Tom.

"Something's turned up and we're going to have to alter our plans a bit!"

And because he knew he couldn't sail without Tom, the Captain had to listen.

An hour later,
darkness had fallen.
But no warning light
shone from the light-
house on the treacherous
Barnacle Reef. Instead
a false light beamed
from a point
further out to sea.

Among the jagged rocks, Cut-throat Jake and his bloodthirsty crew watched . . . and waited . . . and scanned the murky, moonlit sea with greedy eyes.

Time passed . . . tension mounted . . .

Then, from the direction of the harbour a faint shape could be seen approaching through the gloom. At first it was no more than a shadow . . . then at last . . .

Sure enough, a large vessel was coming into sight.

As Jake and his crew crouched excitedly among the rocks they could hear the creaking of the rigging and the swirl of the waves round the bows.

"At any moment now she'll strike the Reef," breathed Jake. "Stand by with your cutlasses, me beauties . . ."

Then suddenly, with
a flicker and a flash . . .

the lamp of the Barnacle
light-house burst alight
above them, and in the
sudden blaze the
horrified ruffians saw . . .

73

. . . the bows of the approaching vessel rise and fall on the waves, then strike on the rocks with a fearful rending crash.

But the name they saw on the prow was NOT *Black Pig*—

for it was Cut-throat Jake's own ship
that had struck the Barnacle Reef!
And for Jake, even worse was to follow.

From the bows of his doomed ship
leapt a score of red-coated militia-men,
with Tom the cabin boy pointing the way
and Captain Pugwash and his crew keeping
well out of harm's way at the back.

Dazzled by the sudden glare, bewildered
by the unexpected turn of events, Jake and
his crew put up little resistance. Very soon
they were rounded up, and marched away . . .

. . . into the light-house, where . . .

Tom's Uncle Joe was released and Jake and his men were put in irons.

"Dashed grateful to you, sir!" said the Officer in Charge to Captain Pugwash, "for leading us to these desperate criminals!"

"Think nothing of it. Glad to be of service . . . especially if there's a reward attached!" replied the Captain, slightly out of breath.

And he boasted all the way, of course . . .

as Tom and his uncle rowed him and the crew
back to the harbour, leaving the militia in
charge of the light-house and the prisoners,
and the *Flying Dustman* firmly stuck
on the rocks.

"Smart work, Tom," whispered Uncle Joe. "I know it was you who fixed it all — but it beats me how you did it."

"Easy, Uncle," said Tom. "When Jake and his crew grabbed you, I first set the lamp to light at about eight this evening in the way you showed me. Then I escaped down the *outside* of the light-house."

"But why didn't your Captain sail out on the evening tide?" interrupted Joe. "How was it that it was *Jake's* ship that went on the rocks?"

"Well," said Tom, in a lowered voice, "the crew of the *Black Pig* really aren't much good at getting the ship going *without* me. So all I had to do was to find out where Jake's ship was moored, tell the Captain to alert the soldiers, and then we all got on board the *Flying Dustman*, cast her loose on the falling tide, and sailed her on to the Barnacle Reef."

"This calls for a celebration," cried Captain Pugwash as they landed from the long-boat and made for the Buccaneers' Arms.

And so, for the second time that day . . .

there were free drinks
all round at the
Captain's expense.

He even ordered a lemonade
for Tom the cabin boy . . .

and told everybody how brave he, Captain Pugwash, had been in leading the militia in their attack on the wreckers of Barnacle Reef.

So a merry evening was had by all, and it was not until the following day . . .

that the *Black Pig* at last set out on the
Captain's voyage to the Indies. Cut-throat
Jake and his men were safely in the town
gaol, awaiting trial for attempted wrecking,
and as there was indeed a reward for Jake's
capture, Pugwash was even better off than
he had been before.

"'Bye-bye, Tom!" shouted Uncle Joe from the top of the Barnacle light-house. "Have a good journey! You *ought* to be all right with a skilful Captain like yours!"

"Smart fellow, your uncle!" said Captain Pugwash as he steered the ship well clear of the Reef.

"Knows a good man when he sees one . . .
eh?"

But even at that distance Tom could see
that his uncle was winking, and he waved
and smiled . . . and said nothing.

JOHN RYAN

was born in Edinburgh and spent
his early childhood in Turkey and Morocco
before moving to England, where he worked for
seven years as Assistant Art Master of Harrow School.
Captain Pugwash first set sail over 50 years ago
as a strip cartoon. Since then he has featured in books,
films and theatres all over the world. Before his death
in 2009 aged 88, John lived in Rye, Kent, the home
of smugglers in years gone by, with his wife Priscilla,
who is also an artist. He has three children and
a regular crew of grandchildren.

Also available from Frances Lincoln Children's Books

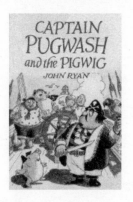

Captain Pugwash and the Pigwig
John Ryan

Here are four hilarious stories about the
greedy, cowardly, silly Captain Pugwash and
his pirate crew, with their faithful cabin boy Tom.
Ideal for first solo reading, they see the crew
becoming vegetarian, their enemy Cut-Throat Jake
being defeated by a parrot, a fierce battle on the
poop deck, and the pirates finding a whole new way
to walk the plank. Full of John Ryan's trademark
comedy, this is a delightful addition to the classic
Captain Pugwash series.

Captain Pugwash
John Ryan
With audiobook read by Jim Broadbent

"Pugwash's crew is as endearing as they are inept:
about as far from the real pirates of the eighteenth
century as a stuffed tiger is from the real thing.
Captain Pugwash is good clean fun."
– *1001 Children's Books You Must Read
Before You Grow Up* by Julia Eccleshare

"The distinctive illustrations are lively, quirky
and full of fun and add to the straightforward
and tongue-in-cheek, amusing text. Added to this
is the CD of the story narrated by Jim Broadbent's
warm tones and accompanied by a very jolly
sailor's hornpipe. Certain to be enjoyed by
readers and listeners of all ages." – *Carousel*

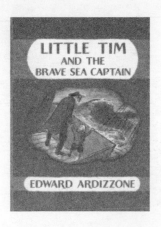

Little Tim and the Brave Sea Captain
Edward Ardizzone

"Tim has the sort of adventures that every
child needs, unshakably rooted in the real world,
but unhampered by interference from anxious adults.
His stirring but comforting maritime experiences
are those a child might dream of – full of storms,
shipwrecks and fascinating knots. He deals doggedly
with dangers, never stints on chores below deck
and always gets home after the voyage.
– *1001 Children's Books You Must Read
Before You Grow Up* by Julia Eccleshare